WHAT'S NEW SCOOBY-DOO?
A Junior Chapter Book

THE ROLLER GHOSTER

Written by Joy Brewster

WORLDWIDE PUBLISHING ™

SCHOLASTIC INC.
New York   Toronto   London   Auckland   Sydney
Mexico City   New Delhi   Hong Kong   Buenos Aires

ISBN 0-439-70128-7

Designed by Maria Stasavage

12 11 10 9 8 7 6 5 4 3 2 1   4 5 6 7 8/0

Special thanks to Duendes del Sur
for cover and interior illustrations.

Printed in the U.S.A.
First printing, September 2004

Chapter 1

"Whoaaaa!" yelled Shaggy and Scooby. They were in the back of the Mystery Machine. Shaggy was playing a video game. "This roller-coaster game is, like, totally real!"

"Thank goodness for that game," Fred told Daphne and Velma. "That's how Shaggy won the roller-coaster design contest. And we got free tickets to Thrill Rides!"

"The best part of the prize is, I

get to meet Chris and Terry," Shaggy said.

"Who are they?" Velma asked.

"Chris and Terry!" Shaggy cried. "They designed the park!"

The Mystery Machine drove through the gates of Thrill Rides Amusement Park. Shaggy and Scooby stared out the window.

"That must be the Sling Shot!" cried Shaggy. It was a huge bungee jump ride. Up ahead they could see kids in skydiving gear. They were getting ready for the Sky Ride.

"Like, this is extreme with a capital X," Shaggy said.

The Mystery Machine pulled into the parking lot. The gang

piled out. Two girls were waiting for them.

"Welcome to Thrill Rides!" called one of the girls. Her brown hair bounced as she ran over.

"Shaggy, right?" she said. "And these must be your friends."

The other girl walked up slowly. She looked like the first girl, but had spiky green hair. "Congratulations on winning the 'Design Your Own Roller Coaster' contest," she said. She sounded bored.

"We're building your design right here in the park!" Terry said. "Want to see?"

"When do we get to meet Chris and Terry?" Shaggy asked. "Those guys are my heroes."

The girl with the green hair spoke up. "I'm Chris," she said. "That's my sister, Terry."

"Hunh?" Scooby said.

"You mean, you guys are girls?" Shaggy added.

"That's cool!" Daphne said.

"These passes will get you into every ride in the park," Terry said. "And the food court, too."

Shaggy liked the sound of that. "Like, free food! All right!"

Scooby rubbed his tummy and giggled.

Terry took Shaggy's arm. "Let's go see your ride. It's almost done."

"Scooby and I will catch up with you guys later!" Shaggy yelled to the rest of the gang.

like, saved the sub!"

Scooby leaned over and ate the entire sub in one bite.

"Hey!" Shaggy cried.

"Rummy!" Scooby said, licking his lips.

Chris and Terry looked at each other and shook their heads.

Chapter 3

"I can't wait to go skydiving!" Fred said. He, Daphne, and Velma were going on the Sky Ride.

"What do you mean you have to be at least this tall to ride?" cried a little boy. His backpack said "Eddie" on it.

"I don't make the rules, kid," the ticket taker said. "Sorry."

"It's not fair!" Eddie pouted. He marched away.

"The Roller Ghoster!" the ticket taker screamed. "It's real!" He ran away as fast as he could.

The Roller Ghoster hit the control panel with its sharp claws. Sparks flew everywhere.

Back inside the Sky Ride, Velma knew something was wrong. The floor was sliding away. There was nothing between them and the giant fan blades. "Jinkies, look!" she cried. "The floor!"

"That's not all!" yelled Daphne. "The fan's slowing down!"

The blades were turning slower and slower. There wasn't enough wind to keep them in the air. Velma, Fred, and Daphne began to fall!

Chapter 4

"AAAAAHHHH!" the kids screamed.

Velma had an idea. "We've got to jam the fan!"

"But how?!" Fred shouted.

"I know!" Daphne yelled. She grabbed her belt and threw it down into the fan. The belt twisted around the blades until the fan stopped.

Daphne, Fred, and Velma fell

"I never cared for these fancy new rides, anyway," said Sam. "Bungee jumping, skydiving? These new rides are too dangerous. The old rides were better."

Fred turned to Daphne and Velma. "Well, girls. It looks like we've got a mystery on our hands! Let's split up. Velma, you go see if Chris and Terry know anything about this 'Roller Ghoster.'"

Daphne nodded. "Right! And Fred and I will take a look at some of these rides."

"Strange things have been happening here, kids," Sam warned. "If you're not careful, the next ride could be your last!"

Chapter 5

"Terry? Chris?" Shaggy called. "Yoohoo?"

Shaggy and Scooby had lost the sisters during their park tour. "Looks like they forgot us, Scoob," Shaggy said. "Wanna hit some rides until they show up again?"

"Rokay," Scooby nodded.

"Let's check out that one!" Shaggy said, pointing up at the Sling Shot.

The ball dropped off the tower and started falling. The rope stretched farther and farther, but the ball slowed down. It stopped right before it touched the ground.

"See, Scoob?" smiled Shaggy. "That wasn't so . . ."

Just then, the rope snapped back. It flung the ball back up into the air.

". . . baaaaad!" yelled Shaggy.

The ball flew past the top of the tower. But suddenly, the rope snapped. The ball soared across the amusement park and bounced off the Sky Ride. *BOING!*

"Heeeeeeelp!" cried Scooby and Shaggy.

Chapter 6

On the other side of the park, Velma was knocking on the door to the park office. "Hello?"

There was no answer. Velma opened the door. Two desks sat on opposite sides of the office.

"Terry? Chris? Are you here?" Velma asked. She noticed a hairbrush on one desk. There were some green hairs stuck in it.

"Velma?" It was Terry.

"Oh, there you are," Velma said.
"I was looking for you."

"What's wrong?" Terry asked.

"One of your rides almost made
a salad out of my friends and me,"
Velma explained.

"Oh no!" Terry cried. "The Roller
Ghoster?"

A man with a video camera

burst into the office. Chris was right behind him, looking angry.

"This is Harry Harrison, reporter," the man began. "I'm here at Thrill Rides Amusement Park. I'm talking to Chris about rumors that the park is haunted."

Chris was mad. "How many times do I have to tell you?" she yelled. "It's NOT haunted!"

"How do YOU explain all the accidents?" Harry asked Terry.

"We're very sorry," Terry explained. "We're doing everything we can to make the rides safe."

Meanwhile, out in the park, the big metal ball was rolling around. Scooby and Shaggy were still trapped inside!

Chapter 7

"Keep running, Scoob!" yelled
Shaggy. Scooby and Shaggy were
trying to slow down the giant ball.
But the ball just rolled faster and
faster. It was heading right toward
a cliff!

Then Shaggy had an idea. "You
think a Scooby Snack would help?"

"Reah-reah-reah!" Scooby said.

Shaggy pulled out a Scooby
Snack and held it in front of

Scooby. Scooby raced for the snack. The faster he ran, the slower the ball rolled. Finally, it stopped right at the edge of the cliff.

Shaggy pulled out another snack. "TWO Scooby Snacks?"

Scooby's eyes popped open. He ran even faster than before.

The ball shot away from the cliff. It smashed into a tree and cracked open. Scooby and Shaggy were finally free!

Daphne, Fred, and Velma ran up to Shaggy and Scooby. "What happened to you guys?" Daphne asked.

Shaggy was a little dizzy. All he could say was, "Monster."

"You saw the Roller Ghoster?"

"But . . ." Velma started. The door shut behind her. A rocket at the back of the ride burst into flames. The ride shot off in a blur.

"Like, look!" cried Shaggy, pointing through the window.

Up ahead on the tracks was the Roller Ghoster. He was using a wrench to mess with the tracks!

"Ruh-roh!" barked Scooby.

It was too late to do anything. The Rocket Coaster jumped the rails and flew into the air!

"Heeeeeeelp!" the gang screamed.

Chapter 8

The Rocket Coaster soared through the air toward the lake. The kids held on for a big SPLASH! But when the rocket hit the water, it just bounced along. It finally stopped near the shore.

Fred forced the doors open and everyone swam out. Chris and Terry met them at the shore. Harry was right behind them.

"Are you guys all right?" Terry

asked.

"My Rocket Coaster!" Chris cried. "It's ruined!"

"Update!" Harry reported. "The Roller Ghoster has struck again!"

Velma was searching for clues. "Look what I found!" she shouted. She held up a wrench.

"What kind of ghost uses a wrench?" Harry asked.

"Like, one that has a screw loose!" Shaggy joked.

Chris grabbed the wrench. "Give me that! It's mine!"

Everyone stared at Chris. "I didn't do it," Chris tried to explain. "It's just my wrench."

"I have an idea," Velma said slowly. "You know this piece of green fur I found? It proves some- thing very important."

"What's that?" asked Fred.

Daphne looked closely at the fur. "Easy! This isn't real fur."

"Which proves the Roller Ghoster is someone in a costume!" Velma exclaimed.

"Someone like Harry?" Chris guessed.

"I need proof," Velma said. "We should take a look at these broken rides. Chris, where do you get them fixed?"

Chapter 9

The gang walked into a large warehouse. Old rides filled the shop, waiting to be fixed. Sam was working on a giant blow-up bouncing tent.

"Sam?" Velma said.

"Now, this was a good ride," Sam said. "It was real fun for the kids. Safe, too, if they didn't jump around too much." He shook his head sadly. "They don't make them like this anymore."

Fred stepped forward. "That's why you did it, isn't it?"

Sam looked surprised. "Did what?"

"You hate new rides," Fred said. "It would be easy for you to break them."

Velma shook her head. "It's not him, Fred," she said. "The rides weren't really broken. They just *looked* broken. Right, Sam?"

"Right!" Sam said. "They looked broken, but when I went to fix them they were safe."

"Aha!" Velma exclaimed. "That means my theory is probably right!" She turned to the rest of the gang. "But we'll need to catch our ghost in the act to be sure."

"I've got just the plan!" Fred said. "All I need is for someone to be the bait."

Everyone turned and looked at Shaggy and Scooby.

"Hey!" Shaggy yelled. "Why's everybody looking at us?"

Chapter 10

Shaggy and Scooby walked
slowly across the park. Chris and
Terry were standing by the park
office. Scooby and Shaggy pretended not to see them, but Shaggy
spoke loud enough for them to
hear. "Well, Scoob, I guess that
wraps up the case . . ."

The next step was to find Harry.
He was sitting at a table fixing his
camera. Shaggy and Scooby acted

like they didn't notice him. "Now that we know who the Roller Ghoster is . . ." said Shaggy loudly.

When they found Eddie and Sam, they finished their act. "There's nothing left to do," Shaggy said. He pretended not to see Eddie and Sam. "I guess we should call the police from the pay phones near the entrance."

Shaggy winked at Scooby. "How did I do?" he whispered.

Scooby just rolled his eyes.

Chapter 11

Shaggy and Scooby waited by the pay phones. "Stay alert, Scooby," Shaggy said. "Now that the Roller Ghoster thinks we're on to him, he'll be after us."

"Rrrrroooooaaarrr!" It was the Roller Ghoster! He was standing right behind Scooby!

Scooby and Shaggy screamed! They both ran into the park. The Roller Ghoster chased after them.

Scooby and Shaggy ran by the Rollerblade stand. Fred, Daphne, and Velma were hiding there with big nets. When the Roller Ghoster ran past, they threw their nets at the monster. But the Roller Ghoster was too fast!

"Keep running, Scoob!" Shaggy yelled. He and Scooby ran into the Skate Shop. When they zipped out the back door, Shaggy was on a skateboard. Scooby had Rollerblades on all four paws.

The Roller Ghoster was still close behind! "Zoinks!" Shaggy yelled, pointing. "Stairs!"

Shaggy's skateboard flew out from under him. He skated down the handrail.

"Ruh-roh!" Scooby barked. He sailed into the air. Then he landed safely at the bottom.

"Rrrroooooooarrr!" The Roller Ghoster was right behind them.

Shaggy skated right for a big pipe in the skatepark. It was too small for him to fit. So he jumped up and let his skateboard roll through the pipe. Shaggy hopped back onto his skateboard at the other end.

Scooby followed him. He spread his legs and bladed right over the pipe.

Last came the Roller Ghoster. It was right on Scooby's tail — but it tripped over the pipe and landed with a big crash!

Chapter 12

"It's all over, Roller Ghoster,"
Fred said. "You left us all the clues
we needed. First you lost your
wrench at the Rocket Coaster."

"That's not all," Daphne said. "It
wasn't real green fur we found at
the SkyRide. It was hair from a
green wig!"

Fred reached for the mask.
"This proves that the Roller
Ghoster is really . . . Chris!"

He pulled off the mask, but it wasn't Chris. "Terry?!" they cried.

"Just as I expected!" Velma exclaimed.

Chris was confused. "But why would my own sister frame me?"

"Maybe because she was jealous?" Velma replied.

"It's true!" yelled Terry. "I always did all the work. I made all your crazy designs into rides, but I never got to build any of my own!"

"I never thought about it like that," Chris said.

"You never thought at all!" Terry cried. "You were easy to frame!"

"Too easy," said Velma. "That's what tripped you up. The wrench was way too obvious a clue."

"And the green fur, green hair thing?" Daphne laughed. "Please!"

"I figured it out when Sam said that the broken rides were still safe," Velma explained. "Terry wanted to make sure no one really got hurt."

"And after her sister was blamed, Terry would control the park," Daphne added. "She could build whatever she wanted."

Terry shook her fist. "I would have gotten away with it, too, if it weren't for you meddling kids!"

"In a way, you did get away with it," Velma said.

"Velma's right!" Fred agreed. "You didn't do anything illegal."

Eddie jumped out from behind the pay phones. "So how come I wasn't a suspect?"

"You're too short to wear the costume!" Velma laughed.

"Aw, man!" Eddie said sadly.

Shaggy looked at Eddie. He had an idea. "You know what you're not too short for?"

A little while later, Shaggy, Scooby, and Eddie were strapped in and ready to ride Snack and

Spin. Shaggy's brand-new ride was finally done!

"Thanks, Shaggy!" Eddie said.

"No problem, pal," said Shaggy.

The car slowly climbed the tracks. "Hold on tight!" Shaggy yelled.

The car dove through the Deviled Egg Drop. Then it swooshed around Chocolate Chunk Curve.

"Aaaaahhh!" Scooby, Shaggy, and Eddie yelled. When they flew over Jelly Bean Jump, the car soared into the air. The tracks had ended! Had the Roller Ghoster struck again?

"Aaaaahhhh!!!" they screamed.

Then a parachute popped open

above the car. Eddie peered over the side of the car and cheered. They were falling into a big bowl of ice cream. "Hey!" he shouted. "We're landing in a giant hot fudge sundae!"

Three spoons suddenly popped up in front of each rider.

"We have to eat our way out!" Shaggy said proudly.

Scooby raised his spoon. "Scooby-Dooby-Doooo!"